KU-753-161

Honeypot Hill

To the City

Saffron Thimble's
Sewing Shop

The Orchards

Paddle Steamer
Quay

Aunt
Marigold
General
Store

Lavender Valley
Garden Centre

Healing House and Garden

The Worthingtons' House

Melody
Maker's
Music Shop

Lavender Lake

Bumble Bee's Teashop

Lavender Lake
School of Dance

SCHOOL

Peppermint
Pond

Hedgerows Hotel
Where Mimosa lives

Rosehip School

Summer Meadow

Christmas Corner

Wildspice Woods

Visit Princess Poppy for fun, games, puzzles, activities, downloads and lots more at:

www.princesspoppy.com

★

THE HOLIDAY
A PICTURE CORGI BOOK 978 0 552 57574 4
First published in Great Britain by Picture Corgi,
an imprint of Random House Children's Publishers UK
A Random House Group Company

This edition published 2013

3 5 7 9 10 8 6 4 2

Text copyright © Janey Louise Jones, 2013
Illustration copyright © Picture Corgi Books, 2013
Illustrations by Veronica Vasylenko
The right of Janey Louise Jones and Veronica Vasylenko to be identified as the author and illustrator of this work has been
asserted in accordance with the Copyright, Designs and Patents Act 1988.

All rights reserved.

Picture Corgi Books are published by Random House Children's Publishers UK,
61–63 Uxbridge Road, London W5 5SA

www.princesspoppy.com
www.randomhousechildrens.co.uk

Addresses for companies within The Random House Group Limited can be found at: www.randomhouse.co.uk/offices.htm

THE RANDOM HOUSE GROUP Limited Reg. No. 954009

A CIP catalogue record for this book is available from the British Library.

Printed in China

Princess Poppy

The Holiday

Written by Janey Louise Jones

PICTURE CORGI

With love to Emilia, an explorer like

Princess Poppy! xx

The Holiday

featuring

Mum

Honey

Dad

Princess Poppy

Klara

Archie

Angel

"I wish you were coming to Portugal with us!" sighed Poppy.

"Me too!" Honey replied.

"Mum says the sea will be really warm and we'll eat loads of seafood," said Poppy.

"Ew, I'm glad I'm not coming then. Seafood's gross!" giggled Honey.

After the plane landed, Poppy and her family collected their suitcases, piled into a hire car and set off for the seaside.

"When will we be there?" whined Poppy impatiently.

"Any minute now," said Dad, "I promise."

The car rounded a sharp bend to
reveal a pretty seaside town.

Dad drove through the narrow cobbled streets towards the harbour and parked outside a guest house.

"We're here!" he announced.

"Wow!" gasped Poppy. "It's amazing."

The next morning they went to explore. It was so different to Honeypot Hill. The air was warm and salty and there were lots of unusual-looking shops and cafés.

"Can we go to that ice-cream parlour?" asked Poppy.

"We've only just had breakfast *and* we're on our way to the beach," laughed Mum. "We'll go another time, I promise."

On the beach Poppy soon got bored.

Mum was trying to keep the twins in check and Dad
had his nose buried in a book.

If only Honey were here, she thought.

But then she noticed a girl of about her age so she went to see if she wanted to play.

The girl's name was Klara, and even though she only spoke a little English and Poppy didn't speak any Dutch, they were soon firm friends.

For the rest of the holiday Poppy and Klara had such fun together.

They swam
in the sea,

built spectacular
sandcastles

and practised
their Portuguese.

They were even allowed to explore the seafront as long as they promised to keep the dolphin fountain in sight.

On market day Mum and Dad took Poppy and the twins into town.

The central square was packed with colourful stalls and crowds of people.

"Wow!" exclaimed Poppy. "There are so many lovely things!"

The twins were hungry so Mum and Dad went to buy them a snack.

The queue was huge and Poppy didn't want to wait.

"Please may I look at some other stalls?" she asked.

"Only if you promise to keep us in sight," agreed Mum.

"I promise," smiled Poppy.

On her way to a jewellery stall she spotted a very bored-looking Klara.

Klara waved, muttered something to her parents, who were also in a queue, then ran over to join Poppy.

"I'm going to buy this necklace for my best friend, Honey!" announced Poppy.

Klara bought one for her best friend too.

The girls whirled around the market looking at all the wonderful things. But they soon felt rather hot.

"Ice cream?" suggested Klara.

"Oooo, yes!" Poppy replied. "I saw an ice-cream parlour on my first day. It was next to a white church."

Klara smiled and pointed to a church tower.

Quite forgetting her promise to Mum, Poppy led the way, keeping the church's bell tower in sight. They skipped down an alley, raced up a side street, turned right and then left, and there was the church.

Back at the market, Poppy and Klara's families had realized the girls were missing.

Frantic with worry, they searched high and low, but there was no sign of them. The girls had vanished.

Meanwhile Poppy and Klara walked right around the outside of the church.

There *was* no ice-cream parlour! What were they going to do?

Poppy had a horrible squirmy feeling in her tummy. She knew they were lost and it was all her fault.

"Um, back to the, um, market," said Klara, trying to sound brave.

They walked this way and that but all the streets looked the same and they kept ending up back at the church. They couldn't even ask for directions because the locals spoke a different language to both of them. It was hopeless.

They sat on the church steps, tears rolling down their cheeks.

Then the church door opened . . .

It was the lady who owned the guest house where Poppy was staying.

"Girls! What are you doing all alone?"

"We were trying to find the ice-cream parlour by the white church," wailed Poppy, "but it's not here."

"But there are many white churches!" the lady said. "We must get you back to your families. They'll be worried."

"Muito obrigada!" sniffed Klara in her best Portuguese. "The market," she explained in broken English.

As the girls were led through the maze of narrow cobbled streets, Poppy's relief turned to worry. Mum and Dad would be so cross.

They soon arrived at the market. Poppy's mum spotted them right away.

"There you are!" she cried. "I've found you!"

Dad and Klara's parents were close behind.

"Promise you won't ever do anything like that again!" scolded Dad.

"I promise!" sobbed Poppy. "I'm really sorry."

"Me too," added Klara.

For the rest of the holiday Poppy and Klara were on their best behaviour.

So, on their last day, Mum decided that they deserved a treat.
They walked into town, past a white church and into . . .

GELADARIA

the ice-cream parlour!

"Thank you!" beamed Poppy. "I didn't think we'd come here."
"Well, I did promise I'd bring you," smiled Mum.

Back home in Honeypot Hill, Dad was helping Poppy stick her holiday photographs in an album.

"I'm sorry I wandered off at the market," said Poppy.

"We make rules to keep you safe," Dad replied, "not to spoil your fun."

"I know," Poppy admitted. "I promise I won't do it again. But at least I got an ice cream in the end!"